Combining astute observation with vivid imagination, Stained Glass Lives shows us stories unfolding in a multitude of colours. From coping with the mortality of beloved parents, to dealing with troubled children, to domestic abuse, to the surreal dreams and stifled hopes we all experience, Louise Worthington weaves wonderful images and engages all of the reader's senses.

Debbi Voisey, writing tutor and mentor, and author of the forthcoming novella-in-flash, *The 10:25*, due to be published in 2021 by *Flash: The International Short-Short Story Press*.

In this collection of short stories and flash fiction, Louise delights us with her dark tales, which take pleasure in the graphic images they conjure up in the reader, for we have all been there, whether we care to admit it or not.

From the macabre to the poignant, we are fed a sumptuous banquet of love, death, betrayal, abuse, unfaithfulness, murder, violence, suicide, despair and troubled mental states. Louise's words wash over the reader in beautiful waves of ebb and flow. She paints such visuals with her flowing sentences of description that they take you right into the heart of each story. Her insight into the flaws of the human condition and the innermost thoughts and feelings , as well as the actions, that human beings are capable of are both authentic and moving.

The collection is filled with poetic prose and beautiful descriptiveness throughout.

Louise Stokes is a novelist and poet whose publications include *Marooned, Faerie Dust and Rescued*. Louise is also a performance poet, playwright and Co-Artistic Director of LouDeemY Productions Theatre, Arts and Multi-Media Company.

Stained Glass Lives

A Collection of Flash Fiction and Short Stories

by

Louise Worthington

Louise Worthington lives in Shropshire with her family. Her short fiction has been published in numerous literary magazines, and she is a reader for Flash Fiction Online.

Her debut novel is called Distorted Days. Stained Glass Lives *is a debut collection of flash fiction and short stories.*

Louise's second novel, a psychological thriller called Rachel's Garden, *will be published by Bloodhound Books in February 2021.*

https://louiseworthington.co.uk/

Contents

Roadkill — 1

Teacher – Listen — 4

After the Will Was Read — 6

The Honeymoon — 8

Jump Start — 10

Bye Then — 12

Spectators — 13

Miss Jones — 15

Anxiety — 17

The Thief — 18

Caffeinated Audience — 25

Crack Cocaine — 27

The House Misses You — 29

Casualty — 30

Homeless — 32

Heedful Nights — 33

Contamination OCD — 34

Winter Sun — 35

Shipwreck — 36

Apples and Chamomile — 40

Role Reversal — 41

Confessions — 42

It Smells Like Rain — 43

When the Woodpecker Left — 45

Reading by Torch-light — 46

Visitors — 47

Maggie's Mum   49
Red Swimsuit   51
Reminisce   55
Seventh Stage   56
Humming   57
Reflections from an Epicure   59
Dreaming Epidermis   61
Trapped   63
Treatment   64
Ryan's Release   67
The Gavel's Sound   70
Beauty   73
It Doesn't Stand to Reason   74
Yours—   75
Chloe   76
Acknowledgements   82

Roadkill

My husband likes blind bends, high hedges. A middle-aged crisis, last year he bought a silver sports car. Take a drive, he said, into the countryside. Sure, I said, and pulled on a gilet. I wanted to wear a headscarf, but his cap made me think twice.

The campion disappears from view, smeared by speed like a finger through white and green oil paint. Studying his profile, I see his attention is focused on the road, so I say nothing, though I'd like to say slow down and ask where the hell we are heading.

The winding miles and the weight of the silence grows until the car eventually pulls over to a passing place. He unbuckles his seat belt with a flourish that is melodramatic for a man of his age. When I look back to this moment, I think I will remember the click and the zip of the seat belt as it retreated into its hiding place and the heavy exhalation of Richard's torso in the bucket sports seat.

Of course, I listen to him. After twenty-six years of marriage, I know when to listen and when to fall deaf, when to feign interest, when to enliven discussion.

Through the window, a still life of a rabbit is chasing its fluffy white tail. I feel a kinship in that dead dark gaze, in the crimson blood leaking from its innards, leaving the memory of its happy life in exposed entrails. Its end here, a passing place and no more. No ceremony. I wonder who first heard its small bones crunch, who dealt that fatal thud, and whether they felt any remorse. If they did, they are long gone.

Beaks will come. Peck over the entrails. Foxes, too, until the rabbit's carcass is spread further afield like headlines and gossip. I see blood spats on the tarmac like Chinese whispers.

Something sensational would be better than simply falling out of love. How terribly tragic and sad and small.

Richard negotiates a U-turn in the lane while I pray for a dimming of the sunlight. In the wing mirror I catch a glimpse of my hair, faded from blonde to moonshine. His wedding ring winks back at the sun as he floors the accelerator with his deck shoe.

The lanes take me back to the young woman I was when I met Richard, a tennis player with a killer serve, to our daughters with bee-stings for breasts and now, to the space that opens up on this nameless road in this ridiculous car. All those years together fade into the view of his rear-view mirror; they are convoluted in the verges of long grass amidst dandelions and daisies. It's spring, I think. That's why. Fool.

I wonder if the rabbit's blood wrapped itself around Richard's sports tyres and is travelling with us back the way we came, all the way to the place we have called home for the last twenty years or so.

When the gravel in our drive sighs with relief because the wheels stop turning, I look at our house and its large windows. I know which rooms are aired, which need dusting. I know which rooms I love and have furnished with great care, which rooms to avoid because I miss our children too much to enter them. I look at Richard's salt-and-pepper hair and I push strands of my own fine hair behind my ears that are pierced with pearls, a wedding present from him.

And then I speak. 'All those nights you assumed I was at home when you were out till late, I was playing tennis with Sheila. The one with the gorgeous muscular legs. We had pink gin afterwards, then we washed each other in the jacuzzi – her legs wrapped around my middle. I came more than once.'

He runs his hands around the leather steering wheel.

'I could have come all night long Richard, but I came home to our bed instead.'

The leather squeaks, expressing his anger proactively. I make him remember he does love me.

'You weren't in our bed, of course. So, I played tennis with myself.'

Tension is in every part of him, even his aura and the fingernails he cut first thing this morning before shaving. His eyes move around my face like a searchlight. It's tempting to tilt my head back a little, or to turn to one side to show my best side. His eyes rove a little longer and deeper on my freckled skin. I wish I had a tennis ball to throw and catch.

'Now,' I say,' take your silly car to a place you've never been to with a woman and set the fucking thing on fire.'

'But—'

'Take your mobile. I'll pick you up.'

I watch the silver car vanish out of sight, happy to see it gone, old enough to know something else will soon replace its fibreglass body.

Teacher – Listen

'Listen,' Miss says, 'to the wind tonguing its way around loose windows in the classroom. It's got muscle.'

Silence grows skin, and I grow goose-bumps because Miss wants us to write about ourselves, to delve into feelings and spit out our hearts.

'Conjure a world away from here!' Miss waves an arm like a wand. She takes a black marker pen, its nib so thick that her words on the board – 'Creative Writing' – even smell masculine to me. Miss knows nothing about me or the place I call home with my father and brother. Miss has it all. All that honeysuckle perfume, fairy-tale ring on her finger and Snow White eye-shadow.

For inspiration, Miss reads aloud something written by a dead bloke. Words billow out as smoke, squeezing a throat and clenching a heart until its faintness is terrifying.

I take a biro in my hand like it's an amulet and feel surprised when ink drips, black as a magpie's tail.

Fat Vinny gets out of his chair forcefully as though he's avoiding a fatal collision. He says it's too hot to concentrate and cracks open the window like he's slamming on the brakes. I hear a muffled half-sigh of air. I know it, like breathing into a pillow to stifle pain, subdue a scream: a cry for help. The rest of my oxygen is on paper.

'It's like a fucking séance in here!' Vinny says.

Miss pretends not to hear, as if 'fucking' is beneath her. She keeps moving slowly around the classroom, performing some kind of ritual that's meant to help us weave spells to build our own palaces.

I conjure a waterfall in slow motion, turning me to liquid, purifying every cell and tissue in my body.

A reckless gust of wind rattles the window to remind us of its muscle. 'The wind's ripped!' Vinny jokes. 'Like me.' And he wobbles the white blubber on his stomach to raise a laugh. His belly button is submerged in the riptide. The motion of flesh drags me out of my waterfall onto a cotton sheet stained the colour of cherries, tomatoes and squashed plums. No amount of washing gets it clean.

If only words could slice the rotten, heal wounded flesh, and hide what can't be undone under a permanent layer of snow. Miss will hear my voice soon, like the wind trapped between sheets of opaque glass.

I title my piece *Dad's Stick of Dynamite* and sit back. Vinny dislikes something about the freeze frame and throws his chair across the room. Paint red as blood spots chips onto the back wall. He grabs my story and swallows it whole. Hungry – as I am – to fill the hole inside.

Choking, Vinny tries to cough up my words. The poison of its content clearly doesn't suit his palate. Miss thumps him on the back with an impressive whack, but still his airwaves are constricted and his bloated red face turns to blue. He jerks forwards, trailing his pudgy hands down the whiteboard, smudging the words 'Creative Writing' Miss wrote less than an hour ago before I knew my power. He lands heavily on the carpet.

Perhaps I do have a voice, after all.

After the Will Was Read

The twin sisters hold each in a violent embrace like two exhausted swimmers. Alice's hands are all over Maggie's face, her neck, scratching and pawing and scraping at her skin in a search for something to give her reason to surface. Anything to feel connected by blood and history to their dead mother and the exclusion from her will, except for the one flimsy object in Maggie's possession.

The thrill of giving and receiving gorgeous violence shocks Maggie, so Alice hits and yanks again and again until she is lost in the sounds of tearing, the touch of slapping. Skin, so much living skin. Toxic and fantastic. The release of anger after months of tending to Mother's needs before her death, the memory of Mother taunting her that she is not good enough to be her own flesh and blood, and the blows she ducked because Mother didn't know who she was.

Now Maggie's hands are weapons. Sweat forms on her brow and above her lip, and saliva thickens at the corners of her mouth. The twins tear at each other's clothes, at ears and noses, seeking flesh and bones, vessels and nails, each remembering Mother at her worst, at her best.

All there is left is rage, and being ravished by rage, and the object in Maggie's pocket. Both women are incensed by the twists of penniless fate that have befallen them. Being touched and gouged is an answer to pain so that, when tomorrow comes, the memory of it will be in yellow and blue thumbprints and red sticky stripes printed on their faces to give shape and hue to a suffering they cannot articulate.

Fat tears of blood roll down Maggie's face where the cuts send the trickles this way and that. Her teeth are red, and the taste of iron is fierce on her tongue – a taste of violence, blackberry-sweet like Mother's jam, like Mother's blood. She imagines it and smiles.

Alice grabs her sister's throat, her ear; she hears the punching of her hands as she tries to rip out Maggie's spotlight.

Collapsed, Maggie looks at the ground where she kneels; she sees the reality of dirt without flinching, and she bathes her striped face in puddles of rainwater. She traces with her finger the cuts on her cheeks where her sister has marked her. The telephone wires above sway vigorously in the breeze, sending a crow into the sky with its black feathers and its drooping claws.

Alice watches the bird like a sermon.

The copper tang in Maggie's mouth makes her hungry for more to answer the fist of grief. She removes the photograph from her pocket to goad her sister. It's a photograph of the three of them, curling in on itself at the edges.

Alice snaps it from Maggie's hand, wipes it clean then tears it in two. 'Take your half,' she spits. 'Mother loved me as much as you.'

The Honeymoon

The carriage clock looks on dust particles floating in the air like champagne bubbles. Streaks on the console table remember where the framed photograph used to be. Now it has been replaced by a postcard of a diamanté sea and a golden beach, propped up against an empty vase.

Through the window, summer flowers in tangerine and citrus clamour for the attention of bees and butterflies and white flowers still cling to the border.

It was a spring wedding. In the framed photograph, Peter and Melissa Lovejoy smile. Her head is held high on a slender perfumed neck, long and white as the lilies in her hand. The rings on her finger shine with gold, diamonds and pearls.

To her left, the chief bridesmaid; to Peter's right, a page boy and his little sister. A pink sash at the girls' waists, blue sash for the boy. The pert flowers in Melissa's bridesmaids' hands are a flutter of cream silk ribbons and fresh smiles, perfectly captured at their moment of doom.

Ordinarily, Melissa wouldn't keep postcards after she's read them.

Where the light catches the sapphire blue waves of the Mediterranean on the postcard, Melissa is reminded of a wink exchanged like currency on her special day. She shivers at the memory. It ripples through her senses: a wink as crisp as a fifty-pound note between her fingers – worth more in euros.

That postcard depicts a perfect beach, fine grains of sand hot to the touch, sneaking into uninvited places between toes, between teeth. Returning to the five-star hotel bedroom, to the bridal suite, with a view of where the sand came from.

The maroon vase is empty. Melissa remembers the flailing broken necks of lilies slumped over its rim, the shrunken heads of orchids, tulips bowed in faded hats. No water to dip, no water to sip. How unkind of her.

One last time she reads the postcard from Peter and her chief bridesmaid, all of one word.

Sorry.

Melissa's nails aren't manicured any more. It is easy to tear it in two.

Jump Start

I was sitting upright, divested of silk blouse and bra for the electrodes, when David's fate was written in electrical impulses. It was a pity for David that my heart didn't shout with the voltage, but the voice of my heart has been getting quieter all this time.

Soon after Beth flew the nest five years ago, I felt chest pains: a heaviness and tightness like wearing a tight belt around my breasts. My arteries had hardened, the blood and oxygen flow gradually getting cut off with every passing day.

I am forty-nine with an old spinster's heart. Don't pity me. I hate pity as much as Pepto-Bismol.

The electrocardiogram confirms the irregularities of my heartbeat. It is not a flat line, but on its way to horizontal. That will surely stand up in a court of law.

I am pleased the nurse sticks to science, for it is the evidence I might need in a case of self-defence. Broken heart syndrome has made part of my heart larger, so my tick is out of step with its tock.

The diagnosis cannot convey longing or the absence of awe, the absence of wonder, the chasm of a shapeless loss. The only thing living inside me is loneliness and a quiet anxiety about when the lovelessness will end – the charade of my marriage and the pain of what might have been.

There is no love from David to feed my heart: this life, this slow turning off of a life-support machine. I want to live.

An autopsy on me would surely prove my innocence.

After dinner at the kitchen table, I am fortified when David hears my diagnosis with the scepticism I expect. Melodramatic, he says, as he dabs his mouth with a linen napkin. Sensitive would be better, but the truth exists in the shadow of my emptiness, and I am beyond caring about the harsh torchlight he shines into my eyes because any minute now he will retire upstairs, take his bath.

His electrocution will jump-start my heart. His will stop. A fair trade.

As he climbs the stairs with a tumbler of whiskey in one hand and the other on the wooden banister, I imagine a lightning storm on its way to the bathroom, cracking and whipping through his veins. Will there be sparks? Static?

He is a little fat around the middle because I am an excellent cook, so it will take a little longer to fry him. Still, a 120-volt hairdryer will send him twitching and gyrating to cardiac arrest until he is sizzling flesh served without garnish.

Upstairs, I decide to put on classical music to add to the atmosphere. From behind the bathroom door, I hear the splash of his white flesh slop into the warm water. His dinner of salmon and new potatoes barely digested. I shall have my strawberries and ice cream later.

I wonder how his face will look when he is electrocuted. I feel the ticking of my heart, and touch my chest to love myself.

Images flash through my mind, a macabre photo album of David's face – only with less skin. The last picture will be my favourite.

Bye Then

I like that the lightning signals the arrival of a storm before it comes. A sharp doorbell ring before the bangs and dousing. Unlike Dad's entrances into my bedroom after midnight.

It seems only right that the scarlet tulips I grew from bulbs are tall, stalky, and their faces look up at the sky in alarm. Like me, they see the storm is on its way and their soft petals cup their own pensive expression like a hand around a chin. Heads too round and heavy with beauty, they nod and stir in the gathering breeze, pathetic and vulnerable. They don't belong here. Not on this patio. In this universe with him. Unable to withstand the twisted blasts that come as we get older, weaker, frailer.

There's comfort in certainty, however sad. Like my dad's gun to my elderly dog's head. Like the first man brave enough – stupid enough – to ask my father's permission to marry me. I loved them both, though that is irrelevant.

The thunder bangs and droplets of rain are forming their soppy defences outside the house but that won't keep me inside. I peek behind the net curtain at the splashing picture. I am wearing my trainers and sports bra. Ready to run.

Dad is snoring on the sofa. His T-shirt is grubby and tight across a bulging stomach that is full of the final meal of chicken and chips that I prepared for him to satisfy his insatiable, appalling appetite.

Bye then, Fucker.

Spectators

Now it's in view, a blur of red, blue, red, blue. Skimming along the track like a stone across a lake. One. Two. Three. A single stretch of sound. Windows, glass, faces. The sun reflects off the windows, the roof. A strip of blue sky is ignorant of what is about to happen.

Max hesitates for a second, then hides in the copse as the train surges past, leaving leaves and litter in its wake. And the decapitated head of his girlfriend.

Max looks at the steel-grey track, edged by undisturbed gravel and steel girders. He begrudges being denied his apology. The ladder of bars fading into the distance reminds him of the bars on his cell window, tainting every single day. There wasn't anything he could do for her; if she wanted to end it, then that was her business. Losing that unborn kid sent her demented. He'd had similar suicidal thoughts himself at the beginning of his sentence.

The passengers on the train carry on to someplace else as if nothing has happened; so will he. They will still chew gum, read the paper, play with their iPhones.

He looks more closely down the line, expecting to see what, he doesn't know.

Ripped up. Human flesh, hair and bones separated like words on a page, punctuated by blood and tissue. Not Ruth but a thing dehumanised in death by the thunder of a train. Her head torn free at the neck, dragged like a mop down the track, sweeping up leaves and gravel with her mermaid's hair. The rest of her body remains on the bank. Her womb, urethra, dysfunctional cervix that he had brutally kicked, destroying their unborn child – that part of her remains intact. Her lower body is unmoved: a runaway who never made it.

Miss Jones

When a handwritten envelope drops onto the hall mat, Miss Jones smiles at her good fortune. This one has a first-class stamp.

It is her habit to gaze through the glass window in the front door in case she glimpses someone skulking away. A Romeo, or an inept postman. The path is empty and the gate is closed.

Handwritten letters have always been her weakness, ever since she started dating all those years ago. She favours blue ink but black is fine, and spelling and punctuation are important.

Clare Jones prefers to think of her maiden name as good fortune rather than commonplace. If she were to write a love letter, it would stand to reason she'd take time to check the address. But love does funny things to a person's intellect.

In Clare's memory box, she keeps an assortment of treasured objects: letters and cards from people who have meant something to each other at one time or another. Once she is dead, Clare doesn't see much point in being buried with her memory box unless there isn't a living soul to give a decent eulogy.

She opens the envelope carefully with a manicured nail, reading it like a famished child. Now she thinks it was a pity to read it in the hall when this letter deserves to be read at leisure on the sofa, or on the chaise longue in her bedroom with a glass of Shiraz. Nevertheless, she remains where she is and reads it over again, letting the words linger on her lips, swilling the most poignant words around the glass of her mouth until they stain her teeth.

The pain and purity of the sentiment move her, that and the curvaceous shapes of letters formed into syllables and words of suffering and longing, all quite eloquent and moving in this particular love letter.

Dear Lucinda,

A name she hasn't come across before.

Clare smells the envelope and the letter to savour the man's suffering. Her memory box has room for one more.

Anxiety

No one can hear the bees but me. A cloud of hot voices gasp for air because they are maddened by containment in my brain, fed on sticky, undigested matter. A tyranny of half-formed slaves to distorted thinking, marinated in isolation. Together, the bees are a roaring disharmony, a swarming mass, intense and incensed, glueing me to the armchair where I long for a honey lullaby to put them to sleep, to let me be.

The Thief

There are regular customers that I don't click with. For some time, Caroline was one of them. It wasn't the fact that she was silent that got under my skin; I enjoy quiet as much as the next person.

At first, I thought it was because of the androgynous clothing: a tweed jacket and thick green cords. The cords were so long that she'd tucked them into a pair of walking socks stuffed into a pair of pumps. She was a petite woman, with hands and feet that moved all the while like blue tits around a bird table. Carrying all that old man tweed and cord around must have taken some effort. It was plain odd.

The first time, she nursed a curler set on her knee in the back of my cab. I hadn't seen one of those in years. My mother had one. The next week, it was a homemade trifle in a cut-glass bowl. I found hundreds and thousands on the back seat like lost worry beads. The next time, a framed painting of a seaside and a pier – Brighton, I thought, but I could be wrong. I never much liked the sea.

It was the week after that we got talking, when she asked if she could carry a plant in the back seat with her.

'What kind, duck?' I asked, more being nosy than worrying about my upholstery. I like plants.

'Lavender. It's in a pot. In a plastic bag.' She stood on the grey pavement beside my open car window and held it up so I could see it. Her tiny hands were wrapped carefully around the middle of the pink pot like it was a baby. Her cherry front door framed her.

I could see in her eyes that she was desperate for it to get in the car with her. So, I said, 'No problem,' and closed my window. I couldn't prolong the agony.

Caroline nursed the plant on her knee like it might wriggle away from her. Each time I glanced in the rear-view mirror, she had her face in it, her little beak of a nose buried in its scent. She and that plant seemed to whisper to one another all the way there. We all have our secrets. Hers was in the plant that day. She had donned a tweed cap to go with the ensemble that week, despite the warm spring weather. After the drop, the smell of lavender travelled around with me like a joyrider.

I didn't used to collect her: for weeks, the fare was drop-off only. A twenty-minute trip from her village, Bomere, through to the outskirts of Nantwich. A scenic route along country lanes, in the main. It would have kept things even if it had stayed like that, but you know how things go.

'I'll only be an hour. I'll pay, of course, if you'd wait. Please.'

So, I did. I parked up outside Sandford Manor and let my meter run. The Cheshire red brick and leaded windows gave the residential care home an elegance that old buildings can have. The grounds, mostly mown grass, wrapped themselves around the manor like a bandage. I could see two residents moving in slow motion around a vegetable patch between lines of cabbages and string. Progress was so slow, they could have been mistaken for scarecrows.

I wished I'd parked somewhere else. I was right in front of a large bay window, a day room of sorts, in which Caroline and presumably her mother were sitting side by side. Floodlit with white light, they were two mannequins in a shop window. It was uncomfortable viewing. I felt like I was gate-crashing something private but with the sound turned down.

I stopped not liking Caroline at that moment. It was the moment I understood why she was wearing men's clothes, the moment I saw that the old lady beside her was dressed the same way.

Caroline had wilted by the time she got in the back of my cab.

Her head drooped like a snowdrop all the way back to her terrace house on St John's Hill. It was like she needed watering. She was all dried up.

When I collected her the following week, she was perky again. We had to stop en route in town. I said it wasn't a problem, but my meter would be running. At Superdrug, she spent nearly fifteen minutes choosing make-up.

We were minutes away from Sandford Manor when she said, 'Shoot!' In the rear-view, her beady-bird eyes were all bright and darty. 'I've forgotten to buy the brushes. We'll have to go back.' She was twitching on the back seat, rustling the plastic bag, glancing out of the window like her gaze might turn the car around.

'I have some in my handbag you can use. Okay, love?' I waited for the panic to go out of her eyes. It seemed to take a while for the words to take effect. I wanted to see the panic go, but it was still swirling around and resisting.

'Yes! I mean, thank you. That's very kind of you.' Then she settled into the back seat again, like she'd been given a lollipop.

Once I'd parked up at Sandford Manor, Caroline surprised me by hopping in beside me in the passenger seat. As I rooted in my tote bag, she nervously rubbed her hands up and down the thick corduroy trousers. She must have been hot in those cords. It was a ridiculous big handbag, making it impossible to find anything quickly.

'My mum was a beauty queen. Miss Cheshire 1973 to 1975.' She spoke in short sentences like she was breathless. Each sentence seemed to come from some secret place. 'I thought she might remember if I do her make-up, her hair. I've got a photo of her to work from.'

She produced it from her bag and held it up like a piece of treasure for me to look at. The young woman at the centre of a crowd, wearing a meringue dress and a tiara, was quite beautiful.

'She's very pretty.' I handed her my blusher brush and an eye-shadow, complete with a small brush. Despite the cab being a roomy saloon, it suddenly felt cramped. I waited for her to get out so I could breathe more easily.

'I'm Caroline,' she said, like she'd given me something precious to hold.

'Sheila.'

'Thank you, Shelia.'

I took a stroll around the grounds to pass the time, to avoid the make-up demonstration and memory treasure hunt inside the bay window. I walked the acres of mown green grass and counted nine benches, all empty and expectant, despite the warm weather. The promise of daffodils nestled under the single oak tree, so I sat there.

Wherever you went, there was a vacancy to the place. Time seemed to be snagged here, a splinter in each fingertip. After a while I got a cramp, so I chose a wooden bench to sit on close to the front door. Sometimes it was uncomfortable having time to think, to be reminded.

Suddenly, Caroline came running out, flapping and screeching. 'Sheila,' she said, like her life depended on it, 'do you have a lipstick?'

I wasn't too keen to share my lipstick with someone else's lips, but I figured I could buy a new one for a few quid. Caroline was paying me more than enough to cover the expense. I delved into my bag and luckily laid my hands on it pretty quickly.

Getting the cosmetic soothed Caroline. 'Why don't you come with me? Mum likes to meet new people. Please.'

I was parched. I figured there might be a cup of tea on offer, so I went inside.

The manor wasn't quite so grand on the inside; like its residents, it had aged and caught a few colds over the years. The bright sunlight and warm day were shut out, banished, and there wasn't a breeze or a hint of spring inside. The tropical temperature came purely from the central heating, which emitted a low wheezing sound. Inside the day room, the bay window let in a magical wish of light that exposed the glitter of dust particles.

There was the wand of a walking stick propped by a wingback chair, and an enormous TV screen. A silent grand piano watched our arrival from the corner of the room, wondering if anyone could remember how to play it.

Caroline's mum, planted in the generous wingback, had had quite a makeover. With her long, slim neck and vibrant make-up, she looked like an amaryllis. 'So nice of you to come. How is Derek?' she asked, like she'd been expecting me all along.

I smiled and hovered, looking for signs of tea. 'Derek?' I looked at Caroline for guidance but found none. 'He's well. Sends his regards.'

Caroline's bird-like hand moved the plum lipstick unsteadily across her mother's thin lips like a crayon. The cerise circles of blusher on top of a multitude of age spots seemed indecent. Her mother's eyeballs peered out blankly from under a rainbow of eye shadow. Draped in cords and a cable-knit cardigan with six brown, wobbly buttons, she looked more drag queen than beauty queen.

Caroline seemed to be enjoying pampering her mum. She had her very own Girl's World.

'Am I ready yet?' her mother asked impatiently, like she was in the wings of a theatre with an audience waiting for her entrance.

Caroline meticulously dabbed at the lipstick she'd smudged onto her mother's false teeth. In her enthusiasm, the rolled-up sleeves of her over-sized jumper had fallen down and now trailed and flapped around. She looked like she was pulling a rabbit out of a hat as she proudly presented her mum with an oval mirror. 'Ta-da!'

'Have I won?' her mother said. 'I won last year.' She took a good look at herself in the mirror. A frail hand reached up to touch her head. Patted it. Frowned. 'Where's my tiara? Did someone steal my tiara?'

The hot-pink nails pointed viciously at Caroline and her bony elbow knocked her walking stick to the ground with a muffled thump. A sheepskin slipper flew off one of her feet across the room and landed on a coffee table, narrowly missing an elderly gentleman asleep on a recliner. The swollen joints in her pointed fingers snarled and growled. 'You! You took it, didn't you? You – what are you doing here? Thief! Get away! Get away!'

I looked at my cab on the other side of the bay window and wished I was inside it. A wink of sunlight on the bonnet caught my eye.

'Get out!' Screeched the plum mouth. 'Get out, thief!'

'Mum! Mum! Please, it's me, Caroline. Mum!' Caroline pleaded and begged, knelt on her knees before her mum, but it made no difference. 'I didn't steal your tiara, mum,' she sobbed.

One of the carers eventually heard the commotion and made soothing sounds that did the trick. There still wasn't any tea on offer. Caroline didn't bother to retrieve the makeup, or my brushes strewn on the hectic olive and copper-coloured carpet, but I didn't care.

We closed the front door behind us quickly, so to keep in the heat. Outside, it surprised me to see a lady on the bench I'd been sitting on. The gentle slope of her shoulders and the cream sunhat perched on the back of her skull reminded me of my own mother, long gone now. She sat so still: she was like a serene painting.

Caroline never spoke on the way home. As I drove, I wound down my window and felt the vivid breeze tussle my silver hair. The fresh air slapped my face and brought me around. I hung my head out of the window a little, opened my mouth wide and drew in big gulps, swallowing them whole. If Caroline noticed, she never said.

I couldn't be hijacked by the putrid silence or the memory of the fetid air or Caroline's desperate pleas for her mum to know her. Time is a thief. She is lawless. Any taxi driver knows that.

Parked up outside the terrace house, Caroline spoke for the first time. The sky was an expectant blue. 'I should have remembered the tiara,' she sobbed. The mop of her mousy hair flopped over her face, muffling the sounds of loss. She was younger than me. Perhaps only forty or so.

'The meter is running,' I said like I was someone else, which is how I felt.

The best of the day was almost stolen. I thought of the vestiges of light I might snatch in the garden, in the greenhouse, before the daylight was kidnapped. I took a look at myself in the rear-view.

Caroline caught my eye in the mirror and held it like a clenched fist.

I didn't turn around when I said what she needed to hear. 'You reminded her, Caroline. Your mum remembered the tiara, the time she was a beauty queen. You made her remember.'

That was the last time I saw her. Beyond my own reflection, I didn't need any more reminders. I passed her weekly business on to another driver. I had to. My meter is running.

Caffeinated Audience

Always at his table before I arrive, Terry likes to update on the peculiarly accelerated growth of the toenails on his right foot. He thinks it's a sign that he is gifted, or at least the right side of him is. I think perhaps his right toes can play the piano or write poetry, things I've wished I could do but don't have the concentration for.

His laughter shows me his teeth. They remind me of a dog I had who gnawed the wall as a puppy, grinding down her teeth prematurely to a shorter, flatter surface. I like that he doesn't care about his teeth, like the dog didn't care about the wall or being beaten.

I couldn't possibly leave the house without a thorough brush, floss, mouth wash and I always have chewing gum in my pocket for close conversations. The minty kind of gum. Especially after coffee. Coffee breath is just too much of a reminder of my maths teacher who never took to me. Nor I to him. Or logic.

That's how it is: you take to some people, not others. I took to Terry despite the age gap. Can't stand the busty feline at the till.

Before Terry leaves the café, he lets his leather belt out a notch because he's eaten too much coffee cake. He stands up, oblivious to the customers, unashamed of the paunch that slips over his belt and stays there, I fall again for his lack of self-consciousness and the towering height of him.

***

The smell of coffee is everywhere. Earthy, pungent, aromatic, wafting from cafes and drive-throughs, from cups cradled in the hands of pedestrians, from my colleagues bent on working through lunch to impress the boss who doesn't know I exist.

Coffee colour, too. I see it in wool coats, in leather shoes and belts. In clothes stores and delicatessens. A leather briefcase on the bus. If I had the cash, a coffee-coloured sofa for two would be nice if it would fit in my bedsit.

***

Terry, and those satisfying slurps he makes while drinking his coffee, make me jealous. Not of her but of that cup and saucer. His hands could be making pottery with the gentle way he touches them. I hate his empty coffee cup that sends him scuttling away.

While the memory of his expression is still fresh, I take out my sketchbook to draw the sitting-down version of Terry. I try to capture his broad shoulders and his elegant finger. More than that, the aura of him. The aroma.

***

The coffee is too hot to drink so I blow on it. I prefer it black with a splash of cold water. Suddenly Terry stands up to push his table further away from mine. It's not especially busy this week; there's just the three of us. The metal legs make a siren screech, which is a little embarrassing. He meets my gaze; holds it. I know those eyebrows so well. They took forever to sketch. But the gaze is as metal-edged as the table legs.

'Bit of privacy wouldn't go amiss. Move over.'

26

Crack Cocaine

It is a raw day in October when Amy catches the train to travel north. There isn't anyone on Platform Five to wave her off, and it feels so cold it is like the autumn sun has been looted. But that doesn't matter. She's made up her mind to see Chris.

Viewing the sliding landscape, like a camera reel on a stranger's iPhone, Amy simply wishes the train would go faster. When the sign for Llangollen station appears, it isn't a sense of being in the right place, more that she has to get off the train before doubt overcomes her.

She looks different. Chris will see that. She *is* different.

Amy's breath lingers in the air like a speech bubble as she surveys the North Wales countryside. She is out of breath from a short walk from the station up the steep incline of the terrace street. In the distance, grey fields are dotted with white as far as she can see. In spring, the ewes will have their lambs. By then, Amy's baby will be born. Healthy and strong, she hopes.

Clutching her loaded womb, she knocks at Chris's front door. The father of her unborn child knows her ugly past habits, but still she has imagined how his face will soften when he sees she is carrying his child. The last time she saw him cataracts of doubt clouded his eyes, but the opaque film will have gone by now, together with the ghost of her addiction. Seeing her clean complexion, her lips free from cracks and blisters, his eyes will smile even before his mouth does.

Amy knocks again, louder this time, and hears footsteps seconds before the front door is opened. 'Is Chris here?' she asks, a half-smile trembling on her lips.

His mother shouts his name like a dirty word from the bottom of the narrow staircase, then turns briskly to face Amy. 'You and your filthy habits aren't welcome here.'

'I've stopped do—'

Chris appears at his mother's side and his face is everything Amy hoped it wouldn't be.

The House Misses You

A wire sculpture of hangers possesses the empty half of the wardrobe. Its doors have been slapped. The duvet is swollen, crumpled from the bags you hastily packed on the bed. Dust will find a forever home on your bedside table.

The sound of your laughter took flight a while ago, a paper plane on the trajectory of summer air. Now it is autumn, and the unflinching mirror in the hall won't retain your damaged look a second longer. Those limp curtains at the bay window can hang all they want in front of stretched raindrops.

Pillows have a memory of a foreign shape.

The cutlery is in the drawer but I'm not hungry any more. All this, as the open fire cradles a scorched goodbye in its hearth.

The house hears me speak.

Sorry.

Casualty

Ella Byer looks in my direction—

Green eyes load, fire from a silenced gun, yet fail to acknowledge me. They search the platform, checking for bombs or perhaps an available bench. She strolls up the platform to read the announcement about the delayed train to Birmingham New Street for a third time. She touches her face nervously where my eyes linger, and turns away.

The shrapnel of three years together splatters on the station platform. A pigeon plops on a memory of Ella and me eating bacon sandwiches in the student union after a heavy night out. Her ponytail was messy, how I liked it.

That mouth is a beautiful still life, just as I remember it, the colour and taste of ripe plums, but she carries herself like she's wearing a shield and her hair is pulled harshly into the prison of a ponytail. There isn't a single fine tendril to soften her pinched expression or to frame her thin features.

She was always too good for someone like me. I have to assume that was why she stopped speaking to me on a Sunday in January. New Year's Day. Then it seemed like she disappeared from university or the universe. They were one and the same back then.

The previous night we drank too much beer then got separated in a circus of bodies at a nightclub on Deansgate. Disoriented by lights and music bending dry-ice into wounds, I gave up trying to find her and limped home to sleep it off. I've hated nightclubs ever since.

I received an envelope through my letterbox the next day

containing the toothbrush and razor I used to leave at her place.

She must see me. Or a ghost.

Homeless

The scared and hysterical get perspective behind the distance of a double-glazed window, under a togged duvet, after the safety valve of unbroken sleep.

Time relaxes in a worn armchair and woes soon ease with the soft support of a footstool.

An onslaught of demands – those histrionics of strangers, a litany of lies and longings – they cease with the opening and closing of the front door.

Full stop to a breathless day.

Neurotic time scales and schizophrenic voices don't stand still to be counted. The crazy monsters aren't under my bed because I haven't got one.

I dream of the certainty of the stair that creaks, the shuffle of post landing on the floor in the hall, coordinates in the ordnance survey of lives that walk on by my abode.

I see people buy scatter cushions, and they see a version of me in a porch to a shop, or sometimes it's a restaurant.

My alarm clock is the bottle opener on each new day. A cork in the fumes of exhaustion and despair.

It's nearing closing time for the shops. Homing pigeons fly. Trolls head to their own bridge and some to a genie in a lamp.

My lights are in this bottle of vodka: a kidney dialysis to replace the lack of a home. An address.

I forget the letters of my name but that doesn't matter. I am no one.

Heedful Nights

Too possessive to be a friend. Demanding to the point of being an acquired taste. He calls my name and expects me to come running. Even if I close my eyes and try to ignore him, I hear him and feel him. God, I hate that.

He never stays in the morning. That side of the bed is empty. Night time is his kingdom; he always likes me best in moonlight, the silhouette of me. Away from crowds. He likes me all to himself.

Touch like a marble floor.

I could sleep inside a hearse. He makes me so very tired, one night after another vigil night.

Tick the fucking clock. Night comes around again, and I dread the pointless bedtime routine. He likes me feeble, broken, weepy, delirious.

If only I could sleep.

Contamination OCD

The release from pain as she holds her hands under the cold tap comes fast and fluid. Together they watch the drops bounce off her red skin into the stainless-steel sink, where they disappear into a swirling afterlife of drains and rivers, a gurgling away of stains and anxieties and pieces of her. Some nights when the skin stings and sings, she thinks her life has been poured down drains, swilled away with water into rivers and seas, frozen into icicles, thawed into dew. She is slowly washing herself away.

He makes strong tea. Her mind drifts in and out of his monologue about tomorrows as the pain comes and goes.

Michael sees the once-pert yellow heads of the daffodils at the kitchen sink. They keep their stalks dipped in an empty vase, sucking up ozone and hope.

Winter Sun

Shop signs advertising January sales reflect on puddles like drunken tea lights. Winter: even the light is discounted to a half-light. Signs shout to buy, to hurry, to act, to dress up, to hope. I fancy another winter coat. Taupe is in fashion.

I do feel the cold. I always have. Looking back, James and I strolled miles apart. More reproach than reach on his part, he recoiled when I sought his warm touch. Wind and snow, a dying spark, you know, I got cold trying for closeness within the bed we shared. We must have warmed each other like wet rocks worn and shaped into friendship.

I see that home décor is on the second floor. It has moved since my last visit. A new duvet cover might brighten up the bedroom. I need a duvet with a thicker tog.

At the till, I see from a display white crockery is still in fashion.

That last night – aromatic candles lit for dinner – a little romance at last, or so I thought. I'd applied soft pink lipstick to frame my smile. Rose Dahlia bought from this very store. But we never saw the candles burn away.

Run away.

That's what the bastard did.

Summer wear is on the third floor. Perhaps winter sun will warm me.

Shipwreck

The shop assistant watches Eliza bend and sniff each kitchen table in turn. She strokes a tabletop like a cat, first with the back of her hand, then her palm. Then she bends and sniffs again.

'Any thoughts?' He tries to suppress a frown, for he is perplexed by this unusual routine that is reminiscent of a mating dance of a bird of paradise, but without the mate. The furniture showroom isn't an obvious choice of location for courtship. 'This is one of our most popular sellers, The Karmen, what you might call an urban dining table. The rectangular glass top with black metal legs is very popular – or it comes with the option of a circular glass table with elegant chrome legs. Or, for a little more money, we have The Casino with an extending table. Great for entertaining.'

'No smell,' Eliza says, smiling as she takes a seat at The Karmen, the cheapest of them all and by far the hardest to sell because of its poor quality.

Is she purring? Or is he?

At The Karmen, she acts out eating with knife and fork, then sipping from a wine glass. She raises her little finger for effect.

'Comfortable chairs, aren't they? They support your back just in the right place,' he says.

Eliza puts down her pretend glass and leans back in the chair. She swings back in it a little, like she used to at school. Something stirs in the back of her mind. A giggle. She swings back a little further and falls backwards like a toppled book.

'Oh, Miss, are you alright?' the assistant asks as he peers down at her from above. 'Here, let me help you up.'

Eliza takes his hand and stands up. She pushes away the imagined creases in her full skirt and pats down her hair. The chair remains on its back like it's had a big night out.

'Sorry about that.' She retrieves the chair and pushes it neatly under the table again. 'This is perfect. When can you deliver it?'

'Follow me. I generally do the deliveries on a Monday.'

***

Eliza leads the assistant into the shell of a kitchen. Aside from a sink, a cooker and a fridge, the room is empty. Two cardboard boxes on the tiled floor are stuffed with cutlery, plates and two glasses.

'Have you just moved in?' he asks.

'Oh no. I'm just getting it how I want it.'

'It's a charming cottage. But the stairs, the banister? Did it have wood rot?' He looks in horror and amazement at the metal ladder to get upstairs.

'Wood rot? Yes, terrible. And the table and chairs got it, too. Shame, but there we are. What did you say your name was? Sorry if I've been rude. I can be a bit preoccupied,' she says, matter-of-factly.

'Max.'

'The back door is probably the easiest way to bring the table through. I'll meet you around the back to let you in.'

Max has never seen so much finely carved wood in a back garden. Oak. Piles of it, shipwrecked. There is even a gull carved into the banister of the beautiful staircase. Many of the stairs have been hacked and chopped. There is a kitchen table and chairs, intact, oak and finely crafted.

Stains have seeped up into the table legs like they'd been syringed and then left to stand in puddles of blood. Lurking in the hedge, oak kitchen cabinets have been attacked by the frost and other elements.

How unappreciative this girl is to mistreat beautiful furniture.

Max makes five journeys to the van. Each trip carries more metal into the house and makes him feel a little angrier, sadder; he's not sure which, when he sees the shipwreck. That wood out there would have had a particular smell once. Now it stinks of damp, of a craft that was wasted on her.

'Can you smell that?' she asks.

He sniffs the air obligingly, expecting a whiff of something in the oven. But Eliza is doing the bending and sniffing routine again at the new kitchen table. He wishes he'd fled after depositing the last chair. Her sniffing and the negligent way she's treated all that oak stokes his anger.

'To be honest, no – I can't smell a thing. Metal doesn't smell. It's dead. It's not like wood that comes from a living thing. Metal comes out of a factory. That dining set is mass produced.'

It begins with waves of sadness, then she hits the rocks and emotions crash and spittle flies. She bobs about for a bit, her arms gesturing this way and that as though she's grappling for a buoy, then she opens her eyes as if she sees the shore.

From her new metal chair, Eliza tells the tale of the murder of her fiancée's memory.

It started with their empty bed on a Sunday morning, then progressed to an empty kitchen chair at the table on Monday night, laid with knife, fork and spoon for a dinner they didn't share. It ended on Saturday, with the bespoke carpentry he'd made being ripped out and deposited bit by bit in the back garden.

A plan in reverse. They didn't dine. They didn't make love. She undid. She unwound.

She sniffs. 'Chris was a carpenter. I'm not seeing anyone just now. I've been too busy with work and the house project to meet anyone new. I will. I mean, I don't miss Chris or anything.'

'I can take the wood away if you want.'

'Would you?' She looks at him like he's granted her a magic wish.

'Sure, I'll take it.' And he thinks eBay, a few grand – easy money. 'No problem.' He resists the urge to rub his hands together.

She smudges chrome-grey eyeliner across her cheek.

Max drives off at speed in his white van. The wood in the back slides from side to side as he motors down the lane, so he slows down. It wouldn't do to hurt it any more.

Apples and Chamomile

Firstly, Alice disorientates the trousers by smacking out the creases, then she hangs them upside down on the washing line.

Next, she makes hostages of his blue shirts by pinning them down by the shoulders, firmly wedging the peg over the cotton so there is permanent tension in the shoulders. The scent on the garments is all her own making, a fresh fragrance of apples and camomile.

Alice sniffs the air. A storm is coming, just as she thought. The sky has never been bigger, wider, darker.

From the kitchen window, she watches the restless wind circling the fabric, the material trying and failing to escape, like a trapped bird flapping against a window seeking sky and cloud when there is only glass.

Alice opens the kitchen window just as the storm comes and rains anarchy on the house and garden, on the cornered garments, tearing shirts and trousers free from the washing line. The rain comes as relentlessly and remorselessly as his lies.

She has packed her suitcase. The washing basket is empty.

Not all of Alice's husband's clothes would fit on the washing line. The rest lie in a heap on the lawn.

He always was insistent on having two of everything.

Role Reversal

Monday

Mum's shopping bags split and the frozen dreams, the pre-cooked hopes, tumble out onto the kitchen floor.

Tuesday

In the bathroom I find her searching in the medicine cabinet peering between the pills, lotions and creams, looking for a miracle to rewind her years.

Wednesday

In the garden, a wheelbarrow precedes her. The claw of arthritic fingers loses its grip on trailing thorns in the shadows of soaring branches she cannot reach.

Thursday

Rearranging the airing cupboard, she finds some warmth in the beach towels hibernating with the summer holidays she almost remembers.

Friday

Spring cleaning, she smears her elbow grease against the windows, trails the up-turned rainbows of her universe, and the complete Os of longing to remember.

Saturday

She conducts the birds with her extendable yellow duster and smiles like a child.

Sunday

I finger the worry beads while Mum passes me the baton.

Confessions

Did she hear right?

The curtains are parted. It is naked black in the bedroom except for a slice of light exposing one hazel eye, the outline of his angular face. Clare knows how soft that eyebrow is to the touch, and how it is to be in the centre of that dark gaze.

Moving to the window, she peers outside. They will never be two names chiselled into a hill, hewn into rock. For months she wished she was that whisper of sunlight on his face. That and no more.

'I'm sorry I'm married,' Mike repeats.

'I heard you. And so am I. Don't be sorry.'

It Smells Like Rain

It smells like rain, except it isn't rain. It's lies. It can't smell like rain all the time.

'You're mistaken,' he says again. 'Deluded.'

Words come to him, then go from him like a wet dog shaking itself free of rain. The drops go flying everywhere. It doesn't matter where, just off, out of the fur.

'Unavoidable,' he says. 'Work. Pressure.'

I am drenched with your words, by your tongue and the shake of your head that sends the wet drops flying at me, into me. Soaking me.

'I hate being late, too,' he says. 'The traffic, the deadlines – one after the other. My boss. You do believe me, don't you?'

When the rain comes, it isn't metal-clean and pure. It is hard and heavy and tainted with sepia-like dye; everything it touches is slightly off. Coloured.

The rain falls on the breakfast table. It falls on the patio and over the garden furniture. It falls so easily, noiselessly; the dripping, the wetting, the leaking of falsehoods, half-truths, lies.

I press my face to the glass to peer out. The rain impairs my view. It is grey. I have dispensed bottles and jam jars inside and out to catch your rain so that when I cry they tinkle back in sympathy.

The rain falters. It is bed time. The rain falls more gently now.

'You are very special,' he says. 'Sorry I was back so late.'

Softer. Still wet, out of the side of your mouth. Making me sip it.

Puddles are beside my side of the bed and yours. In the morning I peel off my wet nightie, trip downstairs and outside to hang it out to dry.

When the Woodpecker Left

To John

Do you still think of me when you see the silver birch across our street? I know you see it from your lounge window as do I from mine, and from your son Teddy's bedroom.

When the silver birch sheds its bark like layers of paper and its thin skin is written on with silk filaments by a perfect spider, does it speak to you?

Remember me for the love letters I didn't write to you once your beautiful child Ted was born, and he needed his daddy to be devoted to him and his mummy. You once said his light-green eyes reminded you of the triangular-shaped leaves, and suddenly my arms felt heavy.

I hope you remember me in the imperfections on the trunk now the tree is older, in the darkened diamond shapes and the fissures of its age spots. Its imperfect signature. The tree matures; branches of its arms grow rough despite closing the distance between us.

It hurts that the bark is white all year round. Its purity mocks our isolation. I want to summon back the woodpecker.

Remember me when the bluebells spring beneath its canopy. Know it is Teddy's birthday and our funeral, all in one tragically beautiful season. In one beautiful tree.

Reading by Torch-light

I was fifteen when I learnt to fly.

It was eight o'clock in the evening when I discovered a vigilante waiting for me in the living room wearing ammunition belts crossed over like a drunken crucifix.

The other one was wearing a Hawaiian necklace of fragrant flowers I couldn't yet smell.

Three others had uninteresting faces.

My choice came. A bulb pushed through rows of soil into my face, the first signs of colour and the promise of scent. It pledged twisted torsos and lemon sun, camouflaged sushi and fine liquor.

I had a duvet over me and a pen-torch to read by. The words on the page pushed something into the side of me like a six-minute stitch. The snake-eye focused on the words, light on light.

Locking doors, turning jangling metal keys, night sounds different to day sounds because my island has expanded.

My heart and mind connected and tethered, then were set free again to eddy in the wind like a kite until Mum shouted at me to switch the bloody light off.

Visitors

Mary and I often sit next to each other in the dayroom. We have a lot in common, what with us both having had one child and losing our husbands to cancer. We are excellent on our feet, so we beat the others to the dayroom to hog the best wingbacks. Rebecca, who relies on a Zimmer frame, said we remind her of holidaymakers pegging their towels to the best sun loungers before breakfast. Not that Rebecca goes on holiday these days.

Visitors come most weeks to see Mary. She prefers to spend time with her daughter Sally and her granddaughter in the visitors' room, which has a tea and coffee machine. Mary says the tea tastes like piss, but she drinks it anyway with extra sugar. I prefer to be outside with my visitor in the grounds of Rose Care Home. There aren't any roses in the garden, but the rhododendrons are stunning in the summer months and the mature oaks brings pleasure.

I settle on a bench in the garden by the thickest of the oak trees while Mary heads to the visitors' room. Not all residents get visitors. Jay is good to me, a regular, and I can't ask for much more at my age. He likes his food, like I did when I was younger. I find the food here is tasty every other day. On Sundays they don't serve a proper Sunday roast like I used to make with Jerry. He saw to the carving and the gravy.

Jay is much more of an opportunist than I am, and he isn't afraid to express himself. Noise. I enjoy listening to him. It's a change from the quietness of my bedroom. I find time passes slowly in silence.

Jay is more nervous during some visits than others. That's just how he his. Mary says her Sally has a twitch in one eye when she gets stressed about getting on an aeroplane. I tell her I understand how it is to worry.

It worries me that Jay's legs are too thin to support his growing body. His tummy is rounder than ever. It doesn't do to fret, though. Jerry said to let nature take its course.

And it did with our baby Jack. We were parents, but only for two short weeks because of Jack's low birth weight. Nature took its course.

Jay pecks at an acorn, hops to another, before flying away.

Maggie's Mum

Thursday

Maggie's mum visits her daughter's terrace house on Tuesdays, stays for an hour or two and makes Maggie's house a home. The magic of her visits lasts for days. Maggie opens drawers and cupboards to find items flat, folded, ordered as if her mum is hiding in there.

Monday

Nasty creases and bulges in Maggie's clothes, towels and bed linen hide and squat on crouching shelves and in low drawers to remind her how inept she is, how alone she is in the universe. The glow worm of the last visit from her mum fades to black as she sits and waits in the dark.

Thursday

In her dream-like state, Maggie thinks she hears floating voices. She thinks her mum is stroking her cheek where a stray hair has fallen, and she believes that once her eyes open she will see her. In a moment, her mum will blow her cheek so the strands of hair will fly away. Then the parchment of Maggie's skin will bloom and heal where she cut herself for contrition.

Sunday

Maggie wakes up with half her body in the airing cupboard. She has found a pillowcase sleeping calmly on top of a pile of hibernating sheets. By repetitively stroking the cotton, the static warms her cut hand right through.

Tuesday

She opens her eyes and gazes into blue eyes. The feel of a hand brushing her cheek lingers; she feels it glowing and a warmth spreading. Waves of relief and love wash over and through her; she is overcome by a rippling and shimmering sensation.

'Is that you, Maggie?'

'Can you hear me?' the paramedic asks.

The day swoons. Blood pumps until her own seams are full, pulsing as if her old skin is too tight to contain it. Filaments of light caress her face like a thousand whispered kisses.

Red Swimsuit

A mother in a red swimsuit closes the toilet cubicle door in the changing rooms and sobs into rough toilet tissue. She thinks no one is listening to her until the slam of a locker shuts her up.

Still wet from the twenty-five-metre swimming pool, the mother wipes tears and chlorinated water from her face. A small puddle forms by her feet on the cold tiles. According to the cleaning schedule on the back of the cubicle door, it was cleaned only a few hours before. The next check of the toilets is due at 3pm. Uncertain precisely what time it is, she thinks it is probably closer to 2pm. She has to collect her daughters from school at 3.30pm. Should she wait for the attendant to come?

Goosebumps rise from her flabby, pale skin like air bubbles in cake mixture. The sight of her body, still slack after giving birth to twins six years before, repels her. She fingers the car key she'd tied to her swimsuit and lodged between her ample breasts like a lucky charm, a talisman.

Teeth chattering. She hears someone in the shower, a toilet flush, the opening of the changing room door to reception, to the car park, to her little car, to her daughters' primary school, to the school gate. Should she just run for it?

The reel of toilet paper is pulled, pulled, in the next-door cubicle. Peering under the gap between the cubicles, she sees sensible shoes with a round toe. Perhaps they belong to an adult, someone sensible and caring.

'Excuse me.'

There is a long pause and then an almighty plop. 'Yes,' the cubicle occupant replies irritably.

'I'm sorry to bother you but when you – when you're finished, would you mind getting an attendant to help me?'

'You alright?'

'I just need someone to come. Please. I'm Emma,' she pleads, and pushes a sob away from her throat like a wedged boiled sweet.

Sobbing now. Nobody comes. No one knocks to see if Emma is alright. She thought the lady in the sensible shoes who took a poo would get help but she didn't, and now she's gone.

'Help!' Emma shouts and stamps her feet on the cold tiled floor like a child having a tantrum.

A maze of gruesome incidents unravels in her mind: her daughters molested, abducted from the school gates, locked in a damp, dark cellar, buried alive.

'Help me!' Emma screams. 'Can anyone hear me?'

She takes a final pee. She is amazed how many she has had since she first sat on the toilet after swimming fifteen lengths. Not expecting to be in the pool for long, she'd hung her clothes on a peg, tucked her trainers neatly underneath the bench. She was gone for maybe half an hour at the most. Even her towel – a beach towel she'd had for the last few years and loved – had been taken.

The ill-fitting swimsuit creeps up her bottom as soon as Emma stands up from the toilet. The rim of the toilet seat is an upturned grin on her wobbly flesh. The smell of chlorine and pine shower gel spice the cold air as she makes her way out of the cubicle.

Knowing it is futile, but doing it anyway, she takes one last look at the bench to see if her clothes, shoes or perhaps just her towel have miraculously reappeared.

She checks each locker, then catches sight of herself in the mirror; her saucer-sized nipples are obscenely pert.

Emma jerks away and opens the door to the reception area before she changes her mind. With one hand on her car key, the other attempting to conceal her breasts and stomach, she jogs through. The tables and chairs for spectators go by in a blur. The glass door to the car park swings open onto freedom with such speed that she rejoices for the absence of her reflection.

The rough tarmac slows her pace and make her body crumple and straighten, crumple and straighten, depending on what is underfoot. She keeps her pale eyes on the target: a red Fiesta parked between a silver Transporter and a blue Mini.

Emma parks her car as close to the school gates as she dares. For ten minutes, the car heater has been on full blast, reducing her nipples and goosebumps to a more respectable size. She is almost ten minutes late, and she hopes most of the parents and children will have cleared off home, but familiar faces are still chatting and smiling and loitering.

She opens the window. 'Hi, Izzy! Hi!' Emma shouts from behind the windscreen of her car.

Izzy is a mother she knows with a daughter of a similar age. Damn her; she carries on chatting. If Emma could get her attention, she might not have to get out of the car. She calls and calls, like a ewe to her roaming lambs.

Emma is tired now, and angry and sad and furious and humiliated. She opens the car door and slams it shut behind her. The cherry-red swimsuit makes its way to school reception like a stray audition from a very local beauty contest.

Her feet are grubby and sore from the tarmac and driving barefoot. She cannot express the shame the criminal who has stolen her clothes has caused her. She sees her feelings reflected in those final few moments on the familiar faces of teachers, parents, children. Whoever has done this to her deserves to die. Slowly and painfully.

The look of relief on her children's faces is swiftly followed by alarm. They gawp at the red swimsuit and a clutch of stray dark pubic hairs. Amongst the stares and sniggers, the youngest one by three minutes begins to cry. Ms Morris, her teacher, consoles her with a rub on the arm and then pulls her cardigan around her as if she feels cold.

'If you've got something to say, Ms Morris, please do,' Emma snaps. 'Keep on staring. Why not? Everyone else is. As you can see, I'm not having an ordinary day.'

'You've left the motor running. Someone is about to steal your car—'

Reminisce

A piece of sheep's wool snags on barbed wire. It remains there, suspended, moving in the wind, soundless, detached from its whole, a gentle reminder of what's been and gone.

Mary pulls her wool coat tighter as the wind plays with her grey hair. January twelfth is the worst day of the year, her older sister's birthday.

The barbed wire is sharp and cold. It takes minutes to free the wool. Mary remembers the sound of her sister's giggles as the wool tumbles and rolls along the grassy bank, skipping along until it submerges in the stream, succumbing to its end.

Seventh Stage

Lion-tamers' strength in his arms belies the fragile mind inside the circus top of his head. Dad's symphony always starts with the flute. Sound grows from a long mellow whimper between his pursed lips to a shout when the trumpets sound, a voice like thunder summoning the gods to rain, to snow, to ice, to thaw, to deluge, to blow hurricanes through houses, to spray mist and douse the world in honey – whatever the conductor summons in his muddled mind.

I remove the washing-up brush from his hand, help Dad into his wingback chair as I sing his favourite lullaby.

Humming

The scissors on the dressing table catch Libby's eye, which means it is day time.

She takes another two pins, thrusts them into the doll's eyes then puts the doll's hand in hers. Hand in hand.

'Come on, Mummy, let's go to the corner shop.'

Libby makes the doll walk across her single bed. Doll has a face full of shiny pins. Next door in the box bedroom, Mummy is working at her sewing table. The hum of the Singer machine is continuous, from morning through to night time. Libby knows not to disturb Mummy when she's busy working, but she is hungry.

She looks at the little pin-cushion doll Mummy made her as if she might tell her what to do. 'Are you hungry, too?'

The humming stops. Libby puts her ear to the bedroom door expecting to hear familiar movements, like the rustle of fabrics, the snip of scissors, the cheerful rattle of the beads and buttons in those special see-through pots, even a scraping of the chair on the wooden floor – something. Mummy likes singing snatches of a song when her mood is happy. Fancy fabric like taffeta and silk for Mummy's special customers make a rich sound, but that doesn't happen very often.

The only sound is Libby's heartbeat and blood rushing through her ears. Loud rumbling in her tummy. She wants to knock.

Libby fingers the poppy-red ribbons in her pigtails. One ribbon is frayed at the end where she has chewed it, but it is still her favourite because of its colour. When it's time to go to school, she'll wear them in her hair and everyone will notice her. Only Libby isn't sure when school starts, or what day it is. She chews the inside of her cheek until a fly lands on the end of her nose.

Fly is tickly, unlike pin-cushion doll who is stuffed with cotton wool and stitched at the seams, made of gingham cotton in pink and red. Left-overs from something or other Mummy made for someone else. Always left-overs and scraps, hand-me-downs. Cold food from the night before, reheated beans, clothes with someone else's name written on the label.

Buzzing Fly is like the hum of the Singer.

Libby knocks on the door, desperate for food and reassurance. 'Mummy?'

Spools of cotton in navy and black roll behind the door on the wooden floorboards, releasing a new and unexpected sound into the little room. As Libby edges inside the box room, she spots a red bead that looks like a splash of blood.

It's a relief to see Mummy at her sewing table, her head resting on the desk for a nap after hours of her machine humming away. No wonder she is exhausted.

The Singer is humming even though Mummy's hands and legs aren't moving. Libby edges closer to the table, sensing something – an odour. She sees the peculiar angle of Mummy's head.

'I'm hungr—'

When Libby screams a swarm of flies, angry at being disturbed from the stinking corpse, enter her mouth. The humming doesn't stop; it gets louder.

More flies crawl over the bleeding head with its pin-cushion face, eye sockets of pins, lips of pins, and in between, a flush of gingham pink and red.

Reflections from an Epicure

It was the spring season when we met. We skipped straight to the dessert: you just know when it's the right thing to do. There's no point in wasting time over canapés and foreplay when you're ravenous for each other. He was spectacular, gorgeous! The veritable icing on all cakes; the big daddy of gateaux. He needed a glasshouse, not a dessert cabinet. Take it from me, when you know what you want you should grab it, devour it, or someone else will.

I didn't crumble, but my first love broke my heart. I was a rhubarb fool. Not that I cried over spilt milk for long. He'd stolen my cherry, but a diet of carbohydrates soon got my blood pumping again. I had my pastry phase. My mornings began with *pain au chocolat* and freshly squeezed orange juice.

Then I met a butcher and for the next five years I was won over with beef. Beef and I were Rupert's muse, with red wine, the finest oyster mushrooms, finely chopped parsley. He cooked with cream, with sticky honey and Madeira sauce.

I gorged on meat. When I was satiated, I became a vegetarian, got thin and lean. Dined on swordfish with lemon and learned to scuba-dive. I loved myself. Loved me and food, and gave up romance for a while. I cooked things for myself I had never contemplated before: honeyed parsnips; paella with the juiciest, fattest prawns and the tenderest of rice; smoked salmon and scrambled eggs with cracked pepper and piping hot coffee. The scents in my kitchen were finer than any perfume I'd worn.

When you live alone, it's sometimes hard to get the shopping right. It does get lonely. Time stretches out. I must have muddled up the best-by dates. It was the eggs that did it.

I poisoned myself. After that, I lost my appetite. I started living on tinned food – even tinned fruit cocktail. It was a sad time. Baked beans. Tinned spotted dick.

My advert in the lonely hearts' column is quite simple.

Wanted. Broth man with dishwasher.

Dreaming Epidermis

Caroline's skin begins to cool on top of the white knotted sheet, and her mouth opens to elicit a sound no other human hears. Tissues are alive, vessels ripe for more inscription as her thought-flesh thrashes in sleep. Now, her skin is permissive, sweat glands and pores open like a mouth of sea-water.

Startled by something, Caroline wakes and purrs with pleasure. Then, with a jolt, she finds her cotton nightie wrapped under her hairy armpits. She yanks the nightie down, appalled by her nakedness and the odour of sweat and something else on her face and neck. Her hair is matted to her forehead, and yet the bedroom doesn't feel unusually warm.

Switching on the sidelight, Caroline casts her green gaze around the ground-floor apartment. A book on the bedside table might settle her down, but the soft marrow of her dream lingers. Her temples ache; the space between her eyes and her legs are damp. Perhaps she should get up, drink a glass of warm milk. A look behind the curtains might reassure her, guided by the orange glow on parked cars and wheelie bins.

Still, the shadows cast by her nightie, the contours of flesh within it, make her pause. The vividness of the dream lingers on her exfoliated epidermis.

She tosses the covers off, now pooled in a lemony light. It is two o'clock in the morning. Too early to get up for work. She decides to do a few jobs in the kitchen, feed the cat, wash up the dishes from her tuna-pasta supper, then go back to bed.

Miniature white light from appliances is cast in rigid digital shapes. The temperature in the kitchen is much cooler. Sweetpea's cat flap is caught in mid-swing – a long furry tail exits.

'Sweetpea?'

Caroline flips on the light switch and screams at the clowder of cats perched on the kitchen units, on the kitchen table, licking at the leftovers on her dinner plate.

'Christ! Get out!'

Nonchalantly, furry heads turn. There is the perusal of feline gaze, but none of the cats move a muscle. Black-and-white fur on the table, two purring tomcats, a tortoiseshell, one mangy moggy, a hissing fat grey male, some mating, some caterwauling.

How long has this been going on? She touches her brow. Is it sweat she feels there, and elsewhere?

Caroline removes the daffodils from the vase and throws the water on the kitchen floor. Hissing, the five cats exit through the cat flap. Outside, cats are yowling and fighting. Sweetpea jumps onto the kitchen unit beside her and studiously begins to lick her hand. Her familiar rough tongue dislodges a memory: the familiar scent, texture.

Screaming now, Caroline runs to the bathroom and hastily steps into the shower. Tears and hot water keep falling until steam billows from floor to ceiling, obscuring the mirror and the face staring into it.

Trapped

Miss Smith touches her neck, expecting her glands to be protruding like loose bolts. Then she checks her glasses are on, convinced she has misread the time again.

Surrounded by the flurry of caged wings, the classroom window might shatter. The door, reinforced with steel, flinches with each of Becky's kicks.

'Cunt. Open the fucking door.'

Once a foetus, Becky is now a grenade.

Miss stands on an island of blue carpet in a sea of paper aeroplanes and broken pens. Her mind combs the walls for inspiration, but she sees nothing in her search except walls.

Treatment

The first treatment room was dedicated to insomniacs. Building on the success of that, Dr Eight opened the De-Sensitization Room and, most recently, the Nature Chamber. Each dedicated space is fully equipped with the latest technology. After a glowing article in *The Nature Review* about Dr Eight's holistic treatment centre and her nurturing approach, she has quite a waiting list.

With extensive residential builds scheduled in and around the town of Kellerton, where her clinic is based, Dr Eight expects demand to continue to grow. The area used to provide open spaces and a vast nature reserve. They were bulldozed after the green belt was abolished and replaced with affordable housing built for different belt sizes: small; medium; large, and super-size for the clinically obese who pay a high premium for the extra space.

The first client, Clare, arrives early and heads straight to the Nature Chamber for her treatment. Dr Eight operates the controls from her office, preferring not to interact too regularly with her clients. She wants to promote their self-reliance and ownership of treatment.

Clare likes to sit in the garden chair rather than lying down on the sun lounger like some of the other clients. The recorded birdsong commences, a melody of a wren, sparrow, robin and a pigeon. Common garden birds, now extinct. Next, the heated lamp is switched on and turns Clare's pasty face a lemony-pink. Lastly, Dr Eight releases a fragrance into the room, a heady combination of aromas similar to roses, lavender, sweet pea and lilies. Pink confetti is blown in through a vent; it looks like cherry blossom being chased by the breeze.

The click of Dr Eight's microphone is unavoidable, which is a pity in the middle of such a natural experience.

'Now close your eyes, Clare, and enjoy the feel of the sun on your skin. Let nature take care of your mental wellbeing. Let it take away the tension in your neck and shoulders. Breathe in the scents. Let your stresses go. You are connected to nature, to people, to your universe.'

Clare waits to feel the fake-sun's warmth dispel a sense of disconnection wrapped around her like a wet cloth.

Robert arrives and hurries into the De-Sensitization Room wearing his usual outfit of a thick grey overcoat and cap. He resembles a bedraggled heron. He keeps his eyes low as he squeezes onto one end of a two-seater settee opposite two plasma screens. It is only his second session at the clinic, and he looks exhausted.

'Take the controls, Robert.'

His trembling hands obediently reach for the X-Box console and the first of several violent games begins. Sweat forms on his brow after a while, so Dr Eight switches the air-conditioning to ice-cold.

'Keep it up. Only another hour,' she says.

Next, the screen gives way to a series of YouTube clips of animal cruelty, sadism and suicide bombings, all on repeat and in slow-motion so he doesn't miss any of the finer details when his attention span is so weak.

Robert cries like a baby, just as he did last night. Babbling, he crawls on the carpet to the far corner of the room and buries his head in his arms.

'Be strong. Feel your resilience grow,' Dr Eight murmurs.

When he refuses to look at the screen a minute longer, Dr Eight turns the volume up on the speakers and projects the sounds that any robust citizen has to cope with daily: a maelstrom of screams and shouts, sirens, dogs barking and howling, horns and ceaseless traffic.

Lost inside his grey overcoat, Robert could be mistaken for a homeless man on a street corner. Dr Eight almost feels compassion for him. She consults her notes to remind herself of his medical history. Then she blanches.

Robert leaves his treatment room first, then Clare comes out of her's moments later. She takes him by the arm to help him down the flight of stairs onto the pavement. His face is grey.

'How's your anxiety?' he asks.

His kind words warm something inside her skin. She half-smiles and shrugs because it doesn't seem so bad now. Clare takes in his enlarged pupils in their hollow eye sockets rimmed by sleepless nights. 'Has the treatment helped you sleep yet?' she asks.

He shakes his head. His eyelids are so heavy that she wants to stroke each lid in turn. 'I'm not sure I'm getting the right treatment.'

Ryan's Release

The door is locked.

Despite growing up in a house that partied all night long, often rammed with strangers, drugs a regular past time, it took Ryan a long time to come to terms with being in close proximity to hundreds of men, mostly addicts. It wasn't just the locked doors, it was the constant reminder that they were locked that echoed in the rattling of keys and clanging of metal doors.

Ryan's ward has three levels with nothing but nets between each level that are there to catch all manner of disgusting objects the inmates like to throw into them. The imprint of the sounds and smells of caged men and wardens are as vivid as his cellmate Trevor on the bunk beneath him.

Despite the close proximity to men, isolation sets in at any time like fog on the moors. He has to be strong-minded to navigate the day and night or his mind plays tricks. Dirty tricks.

Trevor and Ryan share the single pegboard for their photos and other personal items to keep their spirits up and their memories alive. Ryan has plastered his side of the board with pictures of Heidi Vuorela, the Swedish bodybuilder, beside a single photograph of him and his mother taken outside their house drinking tinnies in the sun.

Trevor scurries to retrieve the dog-eared Bible that has fallen off his bunk onto the floor. He places it under his pillow before the guard unlocks the door for their daily exercise in the yard.

Spring has finally arrived, though it will mainly be viewed between high walls and from behind doors with electronic security devices. It would feel pleasant to be outside if it weren't for the hundreds of windows from the cells and the governor's office in front of them, like the eyes of a biased jury.

'What are your plans once you get out?' asks Trevor as they pace the exercise yard under a blue sky.

Ryan dodges a football as it comes hurtling towards him from a small group of inmates at one end of the yard: he can't be sure who kicked it so he walks on, clenching his jaw to hide his anger. Trevor barely notices; he floats along, believing that God has put him in an invisible technicolour dream coat.

Ryan is getting out in a matter of days, so now isn't the time to get in a fight and mess up his release date that's been passed by the parole board.

They settle on a narrow wooden bench as they always do. Routines. They keep them sane. Despite the presence of several hundred men, there is a sense of vacancy about the prison. Perhaps it is the endless concrete that makes it seem empty and expectant like time has snagged itself on the barbed wire. Freedom is a muscle Ryan hasn't been allowed to exercise for a long time. The sky looks mighty big when seen without bars.

He doesn't have an answer for Trevor.

Shouts come from one corner of the yard. A scuffle most likely. Or worse. It is always volatile when the inmates get let out of their cells. An inmate lost the sight of one eye the week before. Ryan looks away, not wanting to get involved or be in a position of being able to snitch.

'You are ready to leave, aren't you?' Trevor asks.

A guard strolls by, a hand on his baton, as Ryan kicks at the cracked concrete beneath his feet. Between the crack a tuft of green, a weed. It looks almost cheerful amongst the uniform grey.

Ryan looks up at the open sky. Will he ever see the world without the filter of wire, toughened glass and steel bars?

He shrugs at the high fence fringed with barbed wire, and the patrol of slow-moving figures in uniform. 'It makes no difference to me. It's the same place, inside my mind.'

Trevor nods his head, knowing guilt and regret won't go away with the opening of a locked door.

The Gavel's Sound

The mug in Clara's hand is chipped and decorated with the words *SHEEP DIP*. Her thin shoulders hunch over the mug and plate of shortbread, so the loud slurp of tea seems to come from behind her.

Outside the farmhouse, whispers of sheep wool remain in the barbed wire around the perimeter of land. Where the bracken overhangs the field, its thorny ends are wrapped with the candy floss of white wool.

'It was good so many folks turned up to support us,' she recalls.

Derek hates seeing the fields empty of sheep, fears his days will merge into months, into years, without the routines the seasons bring – feeding the land, tending to his flock. He barely feels it is autumn. Normally the ram would be at the ewes, marking their back ends with colour when he'd had his way.

Derek opens the catalogue. The cover is emblazoned with the words: *Saturday 3rd September 2018. The retirement sale of the farmhouse, outbuilding, eighty-nine acres, machinery and implements at Heather Brown Farm, Mr and Mrs Derek Tomlins. 10.00 am.*

'Mind you, some came just for the spectacle,' Derek reflects.

'You were a meticulous farmer, took good care of your machines and animals,' Clara says.

Derek flicks through the catalogue. The list starts with the most substantial items: his 1980 John Deere 2140, 7000 hours; old International harvester baler, and faithful 1998 Land Rover 90 Defender TDI, mileage 116,412. His eyes linger over each loved item then move down to the medium-sized equipment: an ironwork sheep race and commodore sheep turnover crate that he's had for more than twenty-five years. Then down to the gates and gateposts, the ruck of pitchforks, some with broken handles.

Derek had felt like a dead man walking at the farm sale. Dropped polystyrene cups choked Clara's borders and flower beds. Old pellets from sheep droppings were snuffled and eaten by the buyers' dogs, pulling like detectives on tightly held leads. The lots had been picked over, bought and loaded onto trailers, driven away for good.

It was what Derek and Clara had planned, and yet he hasn't been able to settle since. Harvey, their faithful sheepdog, is his unwelcome shadow, reminding him of their pointless existence.

'What do I do Clara? I don't know anything else 'cept sheep farmin'.' He holds the sale catalogue in his hand like a eulogy.

'You know me,' she says, taking his paw and kissing his fingers. They are thick and strong from farming, still rough and calloused from hard graft, despite him being retired. The dirt stays put in the scars and creases, the signature of the man, the farmer.

Derek gently strokes Clara's hair then holds her face in his hands as carefully as a newborn lamb. His dark eyes, so dark it seems there isn't a pupil in the iris, look deeply into hers for an answer. He pushes her white hair behind each ear to reveal the softness of her pale blue eyes and delicately lined neck.

Clara pads upstairs, one arthritic hand on the dark-wood banister to steady herself, with Derek close behind. The landing and stairs have been on the dark side since the bulb went years ago but it needs a gymnast to change it. A mixed blessing: the poor light conceals a tired carpet and the cobwebs that lurk in secret corners.

Derek's sheepskin slippers make a shuffling sound across the landing to their bedroom. They follow a well-trodden path, signposted by tracks of threadbare carpet, in the same way that his flock used to make mazy paths across the fields that Derek, with Harvey in tow, strolled when the dew was wet.

The ghosts of their two daughters remain in their old bedrooms, the heavy doors shut, tomb-like cold. They had hung on, enduring the cold winters, hoping one day their children would become mothers and them grandparents. Then the spare rooms would be aired and occupied and the dining-room table laid for more than two.

Lying in bed, wide awake, Derek recalls the sound of the gavel banging over and over again, one lot after another, until everything was sold forevermore.

He knows the sound of the latch on the back door like his own voice; he knows Harvey's barks and whines, the beating of his tail against the seat in the Land Rover, that and the bleating of his flock in all weathers.

He listens. The silence in the farmhouse, the fields and the empty outbuildings is eerie and out of tune. Ever since the sale, he has been surprised to see the grass in the field is still vivid green. He expected it to wither yellow and die.

'Where are you going?' Clara asks, sitting up in bed, startled by his sudden movement and the speed of his exit from the bedroom. She doesn't know what to do.

She hears urgency in the lifting and rattle of the latch and then the back door closing.

What on earth? The man's in his pyjamas. What now?

Clara listens to ghostly silence. Then gunfire sounds.

Derek returns with his rifle in one hand. Relieved and confused, Clara rushes into his arms as he speaks.

'Harvey's come to join us.'

Beauty

I miss the disc in my lower back, the cartilage in my left knee, and the hair that sits in the plug-hole of my shower to remind me of what I have lost. To look at me, you'd think I didn't sleep a wink; frankly, some nights I don't. The lid over one eye has slipped like a tile from a roof I shall never fix. For all that, I have never loved myself more. Parts of me are missing, but you are not one of them.

It Doesn't Stand to Reason

I should be giddy on life. It doesn't stand to reason that I'm not. That's my dad's phrase. Whenever he says it, I see him in the *Mastermind* chair. Black leather and a black question mark on his grey forehead. He doesn't like being wrong. It doesn't stand to reason. No.

It doesn't stand to reason that Mum left us, that Dad lost his cushy job with the council, and we lost our flat and the big telly. I go to school in a uniform for a girl half my age and sleep on the carpet. It doesn't stand to reason.

It doesn't stand to reason that I love and hate the same man, that I spend hours staring at the bedroom ceiling planning my escape, only to check on him next door and kiss him goodbye before trudging to school in shoes a size too small. It doesn't stand to reason. But this is how it is.

Yours—

Not *yours sincerely, yours faithfully, best regards* or *best wishes, kind regards* or *regards.*

Love.

There are half-remembered quotes I would like to repeat to you. I can't remember the way you said them or I said them, but I wish I could.

I have a snapshot of you in a park beside a swing weighted down by iron chains. The sun is in your hair – the tremendous harvest of your hair.

We weren't a story, not a short story. We were unfinished letters and we never knew how to end them. Was I yours, ever? Ever yours?

Chloe

There's a kind of freedom in having nowhere to go. The interview room is perfectly plain and untouched by distraction, as bland as weak tea without milk or sugar, the sort the trainees make when they don't really give a damn.

Sitting here opposite DCI Wine, I view my interior gallery of memories and pluck one out. Chloe running into the sea in a red swimsuit, the white foam at her legs, barking at her flesh to get wetter. I watched under my blue sunhat. It was June.

My terrace house, 47 Tribune Crescent, is on a small estate, tucked away behind the arcades, just a short walk from Talacre beach and the rise and fall of the sand dunes. Chloe loved pelmets, curtains, blinds, wind chimes and bird feeders. It seemed to me that she spent all her time either dressing the house or feeding the birds; there was never enough time for simple things, like a cup of sweet tea and a bourbon.

Now there is nobody to close the curtains or pull the blinds shut against the dark; their slit-like eyes watch me through till morning. The fabrics wait. How do you tell a house to stop mourning? Her touch is everywhere, in the sway of the pelmets, the surge of the curtains and the tap of the blinds. The wind instruments from outside join in with the cruellest lament inside – *she is gone, gone.*

The wind was throttling the wind chime for hours last night, a long, painful death. There was so much fabric moving and remembering her in the storm that I decided to come here to talk to DCI Wine. I'll see what she has to say. You see, I haven't been arrested but have come here of my own free will. The truth is, I'm in no rush to return to the folds and pelmets. The wind will come whether I want it to or not to tap tap tap on the windowpanes.

I flick back to DCI Wine's face, like an eye to a lens, to check I am still in view. DCI Wine centres me. I am in focus. I like that she is watching me and waiting. I sense DCI Wine wants me in her gaze.

I smell the body odour of impatience from the opposite side of the table. Her hair is bobbed and angular, a serious haircut, not like Chloe's. I feel the hard plastic chair on my bony arse and the desire to sleep. I make myself sit upright.

'I'm Chloe White's partner, Bethan Isla.'

'Thanks for responding to our call. I appreciate this might be difficult for you. Would you be willing to confirm the ID?'

The house is already dressed and the bird feeder is full.

I've stopped looking at DCI Wine because she's spreading photographs on the table before me. Photographs of a body, a face, an angle of legs and limbs. Chloe's skin is washed out, bleached, the colour of the small-hours moon. Her rinsed body is under my face, in my gaze, poking at me to look, look, look.

The tilt of her chin told me. The fan of her hair. It used to fan like that on her pillow after a shower, spray out like a lazy firework of gold and red as she read her silly magazines before bed. I can smell her hair, its folds of apricot. Our summer together is in the fibres in her hair, entwined in my hand, folding itself into my arms between my elbow and my bicep. Her hair was so long I could have trapped it there all night and she wouldn't have known. If only she hadn't run away.

I can't bring myself to look at her eyes in the slab of the photograph. Are they closed?

My voice is like a placard. 'I've heard… I've heard she took her own life.' I whisk my gaze across the table. 'Chloe,' I state, like the tide is coming in fast. 'That's Chloe.'

'What can you tell me about Chloe and your relationship, Bethan?'

'Chloe loved to swim in the sea, especially when it was rough. It was last Tuesday when I saw her. Bin day. I guessed she was thinking of leaving me. She kept saying the same thing, over and over.' I sigh. She's going to ask me what it was. 'She said the house is already dressed and the bird feeder is full.'

Reflected in the eyes of DCI Wine, I am a little odd. I see that in her brow, furrowed like ellipsis, the question mark of her eyebrows and the end-stopped purse of those full lips.

'Your wrist is bandaged.'

'Yes, just a burn from the grill pan.' And without thinking, I lift it carefully from the table and place it out of view on my lap. It's broken, but I stay away from medical folk.

I wasn't expecting to see Chloe's corpse caught in colour. The pelmet of her fringe frames her face perfectly. The wind must have whipped its way through the sea, through her hair, into her ears: a tempest, not a wind chime. It must have sounded discordant as it rattled around a tin head.

The sea took her, enfolded her like the expensive silks and taffetas of our bedroom curtains. How perfect an end. The waves pushed her down, down to the dark and the mysterious fathoms of no return. Did she cry out? Did she think of me as she flailed around? She looks queerly beautiful, cleansed right through. I could almost forgive her.

'Does she have any next of kin?'

'Chloe didn't really talk about her family. Her mum and dad split up when she was little.'

I close my eyes and see Chloe sunbathing in a bikini on a yellow towel. The sweat beads on her top lip are pert and so round that I want to pop them. There is sand between my toes and in my teeth. She kicked sand into my face. Her face is laughing, sexy and round, and her mouth is open and ripe with teeth and tongue. She takes my face in her hands and kisses me hard, so hard there is blood on my tongue and on her lip. I wipe it away, taste it, a comma of iron, and it is gone.

The sea is wide and rough beyond us. I want to die at this moment, this perfectly happy moment.

'I'm sorry to tell you that Chloe committed suicide. She left a note with her coat on the beach, so there's nothing suspicious about her death,' DCI Wine says. 'We're here to help you get through this.'

It is possible to look at Chloe's eyes now, open in the oyster of her face. This shot is framed by grey pebbles and pearl shells. There are cataracts in her eyes, it seems, little clouds, the malevolence of her restless heart. The sea washed her through, rinsed her clean of nastiness. She is honest now, in this photograph, on this table, in this room. She belongs to no one but the sea.

I see the kitchen cupboard opened by Chloe's hand and I reach inside for a glass. I hear the door slammed shut onto my hand, a dead, dull sound of wood and bone and flesh. Over and over. I see my wrist hanging limply like a hinge. She is behind the dark folds of hair, the curtain across her face, the pelmet above her eyes and the smile in amongst the hair, the cruel, beautiful smile. She takes my broken wrist in her hand so gently, and smashes it on the table.

I take a closer look at the photograph. I wish I could take it home.

Chloe's feet are webbed in nets, a Gothic embrace: fish nets and fish eyes, glinting scales and tendrils of hair, seaweed. The float of her loose skirt is caught in mid-action, a little octopus skirt, an umbrella upturned. She is caught in the petals of her skirt, in the stamen of her torso; her face is a bud on the white stem of her neck. The whiteness of her skin is moving. I am appalled and enthralled by her final portrait. Beautiful.

The house is already dressed and the bird feeder is full.

'I was walking along the beach. Made it as far as the lighthouse and then meandered in the dunes for a while. I go there all the time.'

From there, I watched. If I hadn't had a broken wrist, I might have dived in to save her. But she'd bent then snapped it. A broken paddle. I remember listening to the thump of the waves slamming against each other like the cupboard door's collision with my skin and bone. A terrible collision. Both so insistent: the waves, the door. Just like her.

The house is already dressed and the bird feeder is full. The house is already dressed and the bird feeder is full.

I remember the churn of the sand and the pebbles, a mixing bowl of sugar and water. The sea foam was like beer on the lip of the shore. Salt bit into the chapped skin on my lips, the little bits I'd gnawed away because I wanted to escape through my own mouth. I watched while she filled her pockets with pebbles. I watched the whole act from beginning to end, and made sure I didn't miss an encore.

The house is already dressed and the bird feeder is full.

I remember the light was flat. The lustre of the day had been and gone. I thought I could hear wind grab Chloe's hair and throw it away, it fighting back, returning, jerking to the side like a flag from her head. Was her mouth moving? I imagined she was talking to someone as she manically collected pebbles from the beach, but I couldn't hear. The wind deafened me, slammed my hearing to the sea and the rocks. Just like her, moments later.

The sea lapped up her back and over her shoulders. The shock of the cold sent her mouth agape. I liked the way she used her arms to make small circles to keep herself upright as the floor slowly vanished. The saltwater licked over her breasts. Her shoulders. Her face. The whirlpool crown of her head.

'Suicide is a kind of crime to those left behind,' DCI Wine says, a little lopsidedly. 'We can organise grief counselling.'

DCI Wine sits back in her chair to take all of me into her vision. The rouge on her cheeks stands to attention on her blanched skin like a clumsy flower drawn by a child's hand. Her face is drawn, a little sad, a wilted poppy.

'I'm alright,' I say.

The room is hot and airless. The air is sour, and the hours have become dry and brittle like old bones. A trainee brings in sweet tea with milk and a bourbon. DCI Wine's voice is gentler now and there is space between her words that wasn't there before. I take a little breather between them.

'I like this room,' I say.

The house is already dressed and the bird feeder is full.

Acknowledgements

Thank you to the editors of the following publications where these stories first appeared, sometimes in earlier versions.

Roadkill – The Blue Nib https://thebluenib.com

Teacher – Listen – Horla http://www.horla.org/

After the Will Was Read – Ariel Chart https://www.arielchart.com/

Anxiety – Paragraph Planet https://www.paragraphplanet.com/

Heedful Nights – Storgy https://storgy.com/

Trapped – Flash Fiction North https://www.flashfictionnorth.com/

Apples and Chamomile – Boston Literary Magazine

Role Reversal – Potato Soup Journal http://potatosoupjournal.com/

Confessions – http://entropy2.com/blogs/100words/

Reminisce – Microfiction Monday

https://microfictionmondaymagazine.com/

Seventh Stage – 101 Words https://101words.org/

Yours – The Drabble https://thedrabble.wordpress.com/

The Thief and Chloe – Scribble, Park Publications http://www.parkpublications.co.uk/